# *Complicated Couplings*
## Four sexy stories about tangled twosomes

*"If You Love Someone"* -- Tara leaves her husband to move in with Nathan, but he abandons her after a few months. When he returns, begging her to take him back, life and love look very different.

*"Commiserate"* -- The same man dumped them both. When they commiserate, they discover more in common than an ex-boyfriend.

*"Passion's Price"* -- Richard steals Gina's heart from three thousand miles away. But, when he moves across the country, her intensity and passion for life drive him away.

*"Lunchtime Lover"* -- Both married, they started their affair with the promise never to fall in love. Then Lisa's divorce becomes final.

I.G. Frederick trades words for cash, specializing in erotic fiction and poetry since 2001. Her erotic short stories appear in Hustler Fantasies, Forum, Fore-play, and Desire Presents, as well as electronic, audio, and print anthologies. Her novels receive high praise from readers, critics, and other authors.

A FemDom, Ms. Frederick, owns the man she adores. Although dominant in the rest of his life, he demonstrates his love by serving as her submissive. Ms. Frederick often writes about finding love in BDSM relationships from the authority of one enjoying that for almost a decade.

http://eroticawriter.net/

Four
sexy
stories
about
tangled
twosomes

*Complicated*
*Couplings*

# I.G. Frederick

*Author of Love Hurts & Cougar Conquests*

*Complicated Couplings*
© **2014 by I.G. Frederick**

ISBN: 978-1937471-27-9

**Pussy Cat Press**
**http://pussycatpress.com/publisher.html/**
**P.O. Box 19764**
**Portland OR 97280**

First published electronically in 2011

"If You Love Someone" first published by *Ravenous Romance*,
December, 2008
"Commiserate" first published by *Foreplay 6*, December, 2010

# If You Love Someone

### By I.G. Frederick

"Stop blubbering, you stupid cow. I can't take your neediness any longer." Nathan stomped out the door with another cardboard carton.

Tara had returned from work to discover stacks of boxes piled up in the front room and Nathan's belongings missing from the cabinets and drawers. Although he had berated her constantly about her inadequacies for the past three months, she had never imagined him moving out.

The front door burst open and Nathan grabbed another box. "I don't know what possessed me to move in with you in the first place. I should have realized if you couldn't satisfy a man as simple as Keith, you'd never meet a poet's needs."

Tara gasped. She had left Keith for Nathan.

Through a blur of tears, she watched the rented truck pull away from the curb. When it turned the corner and drove out of sight, she closed the door, pressed her back against it, and slid to the floor, gripping her arms across her stomach. Her sobs echoed off the floor tiles and reverberated in her head. Pushing herself off the floor, she ran to the bathroom, lifting the toilet seat in time for the porcelain throne to accept the remains of the cookie she had eaten on her coffee break.

When the heaving stopped and only the taste of bile remained, Tara splashed cold water on her face and rinsed out her mouth. She looked in the mirror at the puffy redness surrounding eyes Nathan had once compared to emeralds. Her nose seemed swollen to twice its normal size and streaks of mascara marked her pale skin. Even her hair, pulled back into a severe ponytail, no longer had the golden sheen Nathan had described so eloquently in his poems when they had first met.

"You will survive this, too," she told herself.

She spent the evening rearranging knick-knacks, photographs, kitchen utensils, books, and clothing to fill the holes left when Nathan packed his things. The three-bedroom house had much more room than she needed, but she couldn't bring herself to think about relocating again so soon. They had moved in only six months ago, one week after she received the divorce decree ending her eight-year marriage. Nathan had promised her the love and passion she had never known with Keith. But now, spreading dishes out so they took up more cabinet space, Tara thought about what she had sacrificed for three months of bliss and three months of hell.

"Stop dwelling on the past and look to the future." Pushing out her chin, she resolved to concentrate on the positive. Her job -- she loved working with people who had physical challenges, helping them find employment, places to live, and transportation. Friends  -- she had wonderful friends. They had seen her through marriage counseling, separation, and the exhilaration of Nathan's whirlwind courtship. They had listened to her bemoan the agony of watching him withdraw so that at the end, like with her ex-husband, they had lived as two strangers sharing a house and a loveless bed. And, she had "Hello, Dolly." After years of bit parts and supporting roles at the local community theater, Tara finally had a starring role in the musical that opened in three weeks.

✐

After two curtain calls on opening night, Tara stood in the theater vestibule autographing programs. The stage intoxication wore off, and exhaustion crept through her until she staggered.

"Here." A man's deep voice penetrated the frenzy of a myriad conversations swirling about her, and a strong hand on her elbow guided her to a chair. He offered her a glass of wine, but Tara shook her head. She hadn't eaten supper; between stage jitters and fatigue, she feared even one glass of wine would intoxicate her.

The stranger squatted so his face came into view. Deep-set, brown eyes stared at her from a dark face with just a hint of beard and mustache surrounding full lips. A golden hoop sparkled in his left earlobe and his bristly black hair was cropped short.

"You realize, don't you, that you're much too young to play Dolly Levi?" His smile lit up his entire face, from the dimples that formed in the center of each cheek to the slight crinkle around his eyes.

Tara couldn't help but smile back. "That's why I have to wear all this makeup."

"Even with all the makeup, you still look far too youthful to play an aging spinster."

Another fan thrust a program into Tara's hands. She signed her name and handed it back.

"You were just wonderful," the woman gushed.

"Thanks." Tara signed half a dozen more programs while the crowd trickled out of the theater. Finally, only the other cast members and the stage crew remained scattered about the vestibule. "I should go change out of my costume and get this makeup off. I appreciate your coming to my rescue."

He tilted his head, his dark eyes flitting across her face. "You haven't eaten, have you?"

Tara shook her head. "Stage fright."

"Unnecessary. You put Carol Channing to shame."

Tara felt the heat rising to her cheeks, grateful that the makeup hid her blushing. "Flattery corrupts both the receiver and the giver."

He laughed, a deep, resonant guffaw that brought a smile to Tara's lips. "If I wait for you to change and remove your makeup, will you let me take you out to dinner?"

Tara stared at him. She didn't even know his name.

"I'm Michael." He offered his hand. "Michael Jefferson. I work over at the University. Very trustworthy, I assure you." He winked. "But I don't want to leave you alone until you've eaten. I'm afraid you'll faint on the way home."

Hesitantly, Tara put her palm against his. Its blackness stood out against her pale skin when he wrapped his fingers around her hand. He gave a firm, brief shake, then lifted her hand to his mouth and kissed her fingers. "I'm delighted to make your acquaintance, Miss Levi. I would be most honored if you would accompany me to dinner this evening."

Tara laughed. "You should be up on the stage yourself."

"That's another story. One we can share over dinner." Michael stood and pulled Tara to her feet. With a hand under her elbow, he walked with her to the backstage entrance. "I'll wait for you here. Don't be long."

Much to her dismay, Tara giggled.

The chimes roused Tara from a half-sleep and she glanced at the clock. Who would ring her doorbell at six o'clock on a Sunday morning? Michael turned and snuggled closer. With difficulty, Tara extracted herself from his arms, found her bathrobe, and padded to the door in bare feet. The cold tiles jolted her into full alertness and she stood on tiptoe to look out the peephole at Nathan. Not believing her eyes, she pressed her cheek against the door, trying to get a better view. The chimes tingled again and she opened the door, rather than let Nathan keep ringing and wake Michael.

After three months, Nathan looked as gorgeous as ever -- skin browned by time spent in a tanning booth, hair bleached blond, eyes so blue they reminded her of a cold, clear lake. He wore a sleeveless tank top and tight shorts that showed off muscles toned during visits to the gym four times a week. Despite the pleasure Michael had given her the night before, Tara found herself weak-kneed and longing to have Nathan wrap himself around her.

"Why are you here?" Her voice quavered. She had to remember his cruelty and not let her attraction for him cloud her judgment.

"I made a mistake leaving." His deep bass strummed a chord in her, increasing her desire. "I'm sorry I hurt you, Tara. I've missed you."

She looked up, half expecting to find a moving truck parked in front of the house, but only saw his red Mazda Miata. "Look, Nathan, this isn't a good time. You should have called first."

"I couldn't give you these over the phone." He brought his left hand around from behind his back and handed Tara a grocery-store bouquet of daisies, chrysanthemums, and baby's breath wrapped in clear cellophane.

"Thanks, but this really isn't...."

"There a problem here?" Michael's voice behind her made Tara cringe.

She turned her head just enough to see he wore only a towel wrapped around his waist, showing off his own muscular arms and chest and the star-burst tattoo on his left bicep. "No. No problem. Nathan was just leaving." She plucked the flowers from his fingers. "Thanks so much for bringing these over, Nathan. Give me your number, I'll call you later."

Nathan stood, open-mouthed, not moving or speaking, staring at Michael.

"Your number? Do you have a card?" Nathan always carried cards that he printed out from his computer. He fumbled in the pocket of his shorts, extracted his wallet, and handed her the card. It had one of his haikus printed on the back and his contact information on the front.

"Thanks for the flowers." She closed the door on the glassy-eyed stare of the man she once thought of as her soul mate and turned to face the man who had shared her bed for the past three months.

"Was that your ex-husband or the poet?" Michael took the flowers and walked into the kitchen.

"The poet," Tara whispered.

He unwrapped the flowers and put them in a vase. "You still love him?"

Tara folded her arms under her breasts, and rested her chin on her chest. "I don't know." A tear crept down her cheek. "I know I still have the hots for him, but I don't know about whether I'm still in love with him. When he first left, I kept busy with play rehearsals and work, trying to forget. I guess I never considered the possibility he'd come back."

Michael bent his knees, wrapped his arms around her waist, and stood straight up again so her feet dangled several inches above the floor. "Hots is okay. Doesn't matter where you get your appetite as long as you come home for dinner. But, I don't share." He captured her mouth with his own, working his tongue between her lips.

Tara slid her arms around Michael's neck and eagerly sucked on his tongue, pulling it deep into her mouth. Since Michael had entered her life, she'd relegated memories of Nathan to thoughts best forgotten -- until he showed up on her porch.

Michael pulled his face away from hers. "Love's another story. If you want to get back together with him, I'll get out of the way. But don't come running my way when he leaves

# Table of Contents

you again. I've no patience with women who can't tell the difference between a real man and an abusive wimp. If you expect our relationship to go anywhere, you have to leave everyone else behind."

"I'm so confused. Please, Michael. I don't want to think about this right now. I just want you to make love to me."

Michael stared into her eyes, one brow raised. Tara focused on the deep brown, almost black irises, trying to hide her thoughts that he always read so easily.

"How do you want it, babe?"

Tara hesitated. Nathan never asked to try anything more exotic than anal sex. Keith had been a two-position kind of guy. Michael had introduced her to so much more variety. If Nathan engendered her desire, would vanilla with Michael assuage it? "Bound."

Michael moved his hands down to her ass, boosted her up over his shoulder, and carried her back into the bedroom. He tossed her on the bed, knocking the wind out of her. With practiced moves, he rolled her over while stripping off her robe, and she ended up on her back, naked. Michael reached over her to the floor and pulled up the leather cuff attached by a chain to the bed leg. Within minutes, he had strapped restraints to her wrists and ankles, and she lay spread-eagle across the bed. From the nightstand, he removed a blindfold and a ball gag which he tied into position.

Every inch of her skin alert, Tara waited, the moisture between her legs seeping out onto her ass. She heard the rattle of a chain when he snapped the hooks of it to the rings through her nipples. A month after they started dating, only a week after he had introduced her to the concept of pain increasing pleasure, Michael had asked her if she would consider having them pierced. The idea of a university professor with tats and body piercings, even discreet ones, had taken her aback. But, since she enjoyed playing with his so much, she didn't feel that she could refuse the request.

Tara wriggled with delight, tugging at her bindings,

feeling the chain slither across her chest, the metal cold against her skin. Her breath came in gasps of anticipation. She heard Michael rummaging around in the nightstand again.

She felt the leather flogger caressing her legs and arms. It disappeared for a second and she heard it whistle through the air before it slapped her right breast and she flinched. Again the caress, again the whistle, and then he struck her between her legs. Each time, she never knew how long the caress would last or where the flogger would strike -- along her thighs, on her nipples, the sides of her breasts, the bottom of her feet. She only knew the pain sent delicious shivers through her that invariably collected in her clit.

Michael only delivered physical pain, Tara realized. Unlike Nathan, his words never stung. He never berated her for perceived inadequacies, or complained that she stood between him and his art. With his uncanny ability to read her mind, he always knew when she needed to talk and when she just wanted to sit on the sofa snuggled in his arms. Unlike every man she had ever known, he shared his thoughts and feelings as well as his hopes and ambitions.

Tara writhed from the pain/pleasure, longing for Michael's touch, wanting him inside her. But he toyed with her, building her desire for him to extremes. He grabbed her chain and tugged at it, pulling up her breasts and sending a jolt through her nipples. Tara moaned. Michael had shown her how to push the ball gag out of her mouth with her tongue if she needed to use their safeword to make him stop. She never had, and doubted if she ever would.

Michael bit down on one nipple and Tara moaned again. Her pelvis lifted, moving toward him, seeking him. He smacked her across her nethers with the flogger and she dropped back down on the bed. She remembered how Nathan ignored her for weeks at a time, until she begged him to make love to her, crying from her own need. Michael might make her wait, but the anticipation only heightened the sensation and he never left her unsatisfied.

Pulling the flogger through her slit, Michael let it rest on her clit. She moved, he slapped. Finally, she heard the flogger hit the wall and Michael jammed himself inside her. Arching her back, Tara's entire body shuddered with the shock of her orgasm. He pounded into her and moments later she shuddered again. Four times he brought her to climax and then he withdrew. Tara whimpered. Even though with Nathan she rarely came more than once or twice, Michael seemed to take pride in the number of orgasms he could get out of her. She'd gotten accustomed to coming a half dozen times or more.

Silence ... no movement ... he toyed with her again. She wriggled and he slapped her with the palm of his hand. That just made her want more and she wriggled again. Michael unbuckled the cuffs that bound her ankles, and ran one finger along her shin, across her thigh, and into her slit. She moaned. He straddled her chest and unhooked her wrist cuffs from the chains. She wanted to take him in her mouth, but he didn't remove the ball gag. Instead, he turned her on her stomach and clipped the cuffs together behind her back.

Tara felt the cool ooze of lubricant as Michael guided two fingers inside her ass. He slipped a plastic dildo into her pussy and turned it on vibrate. Then he replaced his fingers with his cock and Tara shuddered again. When Nathan took her in the ass, although Tara enjoyed it, she never came. Now, her trembling hands couldn't support her weight -- Michael pushed her face into the pillows with each thrust. Moaning around the ball gag, Tara kept her backside in the air, the rest of her pushed against the bed. Michael cried out, shuddering himself and bringing Tara to one last climax. They both collapsed on the bed, spooning together on their sides.

Tara turned Nathan's card over and over in her hand. "If you love someone, set him free... If he comes back, he's yours... If he doesn't, he never was," she said aloud. One of her friends had tried to console her with those words when Nathan left. Reaching across her desk for a yellow legal pad, she drew a line from top to bottom down the middle of the page. At the top of one side she wrote "Michael." At the top of the other she wrote "Nathan." Under each name she made a list. The longer she worked at the list, the more obvious the discrepancy.

She picked up the phone.

"Nathan?" she asked, when he answered.

"Who the hell was that black dude at your house Sunday? Shit, you started fucking me before your divorce papers came through, I suppose I shouldn't be surprised you got someone else to rattle your chain the minute I turned my back."

Tara had to hold her hand over her mouth to keep from giggling. If only he knew...

"You left me, Nathan. You said you were done. You hurt me."

"Yeah, well, now you've hurt me back. And with a black man. Satisfied?"

Tara smiled. Yes, she thought. I am satisfied. She found it difficult to reconcile her cat-in-the-cream reaction to Nathan's perceived hurt with her physical attraction to him and her own self-image. But, she realized, Michael was right. Nathan was an abusive wimp and he deserved hurt. Aloud she said in her coldest voice: "I really don't care if you're hurt or not. You left. I went on with my life and that doesn't include you anymore."

The telephone in her hand stayed silent. She took it away from her ear to turn it off when she heard his voice.

"Look, I told you I was sorry I hurt you. I know you can't be serious about dating a black guy. I'm willing to forgive you for having sex with him. Can't you forgive me so we can get back together?"

Tara found it interesting that Nathan brought up Michael's color three times in less than a minute. Although they sometimes encountered racism when they went out together, Michael tolerated disrespect from no one. And after their first few dates, Tara found herself forgetting about that difference when alone with Michael. The subject hadn't even made it on her yellow legal pad list comparing the two men.

"I have no intention of forgiving you, Nathan. You're a selfish, abusive pig," Tara let all the anger at the pain Nathan had caused her spew out in her words. "I don't love you. I don't want you in my life. I've found a real man, someone who loves me for who I am. You can abuse someone else with your pathetic poetry and your inadequate attempts at intimacy. Just don't come by my house again."

Tara didn't wait for Nathan to reply. She pressed the Off button and set the phone down with a smile. Although her words couldn't match his for viciousness, she still enjoyed the thought of Nathan holding the phone horrified that someone had said such awful things to him. Revenge does taste sweetest when it's cold. The phone rang before she could think of any more clichés, and she checked the caller ID.

"Are you psychic, Michael?"

"So I've been told. Did you get rid of the poet?"

"I asked him not to come by here again."

"Good enough. You want to drive over here tonight? I bought a new toy today."

A shiver traveled the length of Tara's spine and she wondered what Michael had found to torture/delight her with this time. She knew better than to ask. "I'll be there in half an hour."

"I want you to wear your coat and a thong and nothing else except shoes." Tara clenched her muscles against the heat between her legs. The phone clicked and the line went dead. Michael knew he didn't have to wait for an answer, that she would arrive stark naked if he asked. She grabbed her coat from the closet and rummaged through her dresser drawer looking for a thong.

# Commiserate

**I.G. Frederick**

Rebecca scanned her spam folder and one subject line caught her eye. "Need to talk about Mark Zellen." She didn't recognize the sender's e-mail address, but Zellen wasn't exactly a common name.

Opening it, she was surprised to find herself greeted by first name. Since she didn't use it as part of her e-mail address, most spam came in using just her last name.

"I'm writing you because we've both dated Mark Zellen," it said. "He and I recently parted ways and I blame myself for our breakup. I was wondering if you'd be willing to meet for coffee one day and answer a few questions I have that might help me come to terms with my loss. Please understand, in no way do I expect this conversation to result in my getting back together with Mark. If you're not willing to discuss this, I completely understand, but I would appreciate it if you would at least let me know that you received my e-mail.

"Thanks very much,

"Sara."

Rebecca scowled. She had worked very hard to forget she had ever known Mark and didn't relish the idea of spending an hour with someone still in mourning for the creep. On the other hand, if she could help another woman understand that he had done her a favor by dumping her ...

It took almost three weeks before Rebecca could find an opening in her schedule that Sara could make. They settled on drinks downtown after work on a Friday evening. Happy hour revelers packed the City Grill and Rebecca wished they had picked another night or at least another location. She was thinking that she would never find Sara based on her description when a perky, petite blonde stepped in front of her.

"Are you Rebecca?"

Rebecca smiled. The woman with long, blond hair stood barely five feet tall, coming up to Rebecca's chin. She wore a form-fitting, lavender camisole which showed off luscious mounds of tanned breasts, white linen slacks, and strappy sandals that revealed delicate toes with painted purple nails. She had a white linen jacket that matched the pants over her arm, but Rebecca had to wonder where Sara worked that permitted such seductive clothing. She herself wore a navy blue, cotton sheath dress with cap sleeves and a scoop neckline that barely revealed her throat, and plain navy pumps. Her only figure-enhancing accessory was a wide cloth belt that cinched her narrow waist.

"Yes, I'm Rebecca. I take it you're Sara?"

The woman smiled back which made her blue eyes sparkle in the bright sun pouring in through the picture windows that lined one wall of the bar. "Shall we see if we can find a table?"

Rebecca nodded and scanned the room. The only table that appeared available, in the far corner, had just one chair. She headed in that direction, snagging a second chair from a threesome at a table for four. The table, with a stack of menus and a pile of napkin-wrapped tableware, probably was not intended for customers. Rebecca set the chair she had claimed across from the one against the wall and offered it to Sara.

"Thanks. And thanks for meeting me. I really appreciate it." Sara sat and folded her hands in front of her on the table. Her fingernails had only clear polish.

"Why did you want to talk about Mark?" Rebecca turned the chair at an angle so she could cross one leg over the other without bumping her knee on the table.

"The breakup upset me a great deal. I thought he was the one. I wanted him to be the one." Sara paused and took a deep breath. "I'm trying to figure out what I did wrong so I don't make the same mistakes again. He talked about you a lot -- you were the one who got away."

Rebecca stared, wide-eyed at Sara. "You've got to be kidding?"

At that moment, a tall slender man in black pants, white shirt, and black apron approached their table. "Let me get these out of your way, ladies." He scooped up the menus in one arm and collected the napkins and tableware into his large hands. "What can I get you to drink?"

"What have you got on tap that's dark?" Rebecca asked.

"Bridgeport porter?"

When Rebecca nodded, the waiter turned to Sara. "And you, miss?"

Rebecca suppressed a smile. The man looked barely legal himself.

"Can I have a Cranberry Mojito?"

"Certainly. Do you mind if I check your ID?"

Sara giggled and Rebecca frowned. She didn't think Sara looked that much younger than she did. Sara held up a driver's license for the waiter. "Oh, my. I would never have guessed. You look so young."

When Sara blushed prettily, Rebecca realized he was flirting. She looked at the waiter again. He had light brown hair that just covered his ears and a mustache that outlined full lips. *Not bad*, Rebecca thought. But if she had to choose which of the two she would rather take home, Sara would win hands down.

When the waiter left, Sara asked: "So, do you mind my asking why you left Mark?"

Rebecca snorted. "He told you that? That slime ball dumped me after he convinced me to do a three-way with him and the woman who used to be my best friend."

This time Sara's eyes grew wide as she stared at Rebecca.

"Frankly, I think he just used me to get to her. They dated for a few months after we broke up, but then her high school sweetheart made it back from Iraq alive and she got together with him again."

The waiter returned with a tray full of drinks. He put coasters in front of each of them before depositing their glasses, then hustled off to deliver the rest.

Rebecca took a swallow of the rich, brown liquid, savoring roasted malt with cocoa tones.

"That's not how he tells it. I always felt that I had to measure up to you. He complained I wasn't adventurous enough." Sara sipped her cranberry red drink and smiled. "Yum."

"The only thing adventurous we ever did was that three-way and he got pissed because Tamara and I spent more time making out with each other than with him." Rebecca took another swig of porter. "I think he wanted us to fulfill a guy fantasy about two women doing some kind of porn flick thing with him. But he wasn't man enough for one of us, never mind both."

Sara had her hands wrapped around the stem of her glass and she stared at it. She whispered, "What was it like?"

"Mark?"

"No, Tamara. I've never, ummm, done anything with another woman."

Rebecca smiled. "Frankly, I prefer women to men. I only got involved with Mark because my folks bought me a membership on one of those online matchmaking sites for Christmas.

They're kind of worried that I haven't gotten married and settled down. Clichéd as it might sound, Mark was convinced he was the man who could turn me straight."

"That's how I met Mark, too. I mean, my parents didn't buy me a membership, but I work in an all-female office and the only men I meet are on the telephone. I thought maybe online, I could meet someone I'd want to marry."

Rebecca sighed. "Is that what you want, to get married?"

Sara shrugged. "I guess. I mean, isn't that what we're all supposed to want? Marriage, children, house in the suburbs?"

"No, thanks." Rebecca shook her head, her straight black hair grazing her shoulders. "I've never liked kids. I enjoy living in the city. And Mark was the last straw for me as far as men are concerned."

"I thought he and I had something special." Sara's eyes watered up and a single tear clung to her sandy-colored lashes.

"Why'd you think that?"

Sara shrugged. "He used to call me at work, just to tell me that he loved me. He would leave sweet notes on my windshield."

"Yeah, he did all that when we were together. Until he got what he wanted. What did he want from you?"

Pink bloomed on Sara's cheeks and spread down her neck. "The same thing. Only I just couldn't ... I mean, maybe if he wasn't ... I just didn't..." She picked up her drink, only took a sip, but kept the glass pressed against her lips.

"Have you ever been attracted to another woman?" Rebecca figured she knew the answer, but asked anyway.

Sara finally put her glass down. "Once, a long time ago. But, I definitely was <u>not</u> attracted to the woman Mark wanted to ... and well, what he wanted us to do ... I mean I've never done anything with more than one person involved." The pink had turned to red and Sara put her palms against her cheeks. "I'm blushing, aren't I?"

Rebecca laughed. "You look sweet when you blush."

Sara looked up with a deer in the headlights expression. "Oh, my."

"Don't worry. Yes, I find you very attractive. No, I'm not going to seduce you and get you to do depraved things against your better judgment."

Sara stared at her drink and whispered. "But, what if I wanted you to? Seduce me, I mean."

Rebecca lifted Sara's hand and turning it over pressed her lips to the soft skin over the pulse at Sara's wrist. "It would be my pleasure."

Sara smiled without looking up. "So, you don't think if I'd agreed to do what Mark wanted ..."

"Mark is scum. He thinks he's some kind of Adonis and uses women until someone he finds more attractive comes along. You're much better off without him." Rebecca took a long swallow of the rich porter. Somehow, it tasted even better now.

"He could be charming when he wanted to." Sara turned her glass around and around on the coaster.

"And, he turned off the charm whenever you wouldn't go along with whatever he wanted, didn't he?" Rebecca raised one eyebrow.

Sara pressed her lips together and nodded.

"And anytime the two of you argued it was always your fault." Rebecca ran her fingers gently up and down the other woman's arm, watching goose bumps erupt at her touch.

Again, Sara nodded.

"How many times did he threaten to dump you before he actually did?"

Sara looked up, startled. She shrugged. "I lost count." She drank half of what was left in her glass. "Okay, you're right. Let's not talk about Mark any more. What kind of work do you do?"

Rebecca laughed. "I work in the mayor's office."

Sara's eyes grew wide again. "Mark said you were an attorney."

"I have a law degree. Never used it. How'd you find me anyway?"

This time Sara laughed. "Google. I wondered why you had a city e-mail address. You must keep a pretty low profile, though. Didn't turn up anything about what kind of position you have. How long have you been at city hall?"

"About eight years. You really want to discuss career paths or would you like to get a little more personal?" Rebecca picked up Sara's hand again, but this time she ran the tip of her tongue along one finger after another.

Sara shivered and her chest heaved. "You know I've never done anything like this before?"

"You know that's part of what makes it hot?"

Sara opened her white handbag, extracted a twenty dollar bill and dropped it on the table. Rebecca laced her fingers together with Sara's and led her through the crowded bar to the elevator. They lucked into an empty one and Rebecca kissed Sara's neck just behind her ear. "How did you get here?"

"Streetcar."

"I only live about six blocks away." Rebecca nibbled on Sara's earlobe, careful not to dislodge the opal earring. When the elevator doors opened, Rebecca draped one arm across Sara's shoulder and, to her delight, Sara put an arm around Rebecca's waist. They walked along Fifth Street to Flanders and only encountered one hostile stranger. *Gotta love Portland*, Rebecca thought.

When they entered her fourth floor apartment, Rebecca dropped her handbag on the table against the wall of the entry. Sara did the same, hung her jacket on the bentwood coat tree next to the table, then followed Rebecca into the living room.

"You want another drink?"

"Thanks, but I'm already feeling kind of tipsy."

Rebecca turned and pulled Sara into her arms. "You know that's probably not the alcohol?"

Sara slid her hands behind Rebecca's waist and cradled her head against Rebecca's breasts. "Uh, huh."

Rebecca stroked Sara's silky soft hair then lifted her chin with one hand and brought her lips down almost close enough to touch. She smiled when Sara tilted her head, straining to make contact. Rebecca relented and they pressed their lips together. Sara tasted of mint, lime, and cranberry. Their heavy breathing filled the stillness of the apartment.

One hand tangled in Sara's hair, Rebecca trailed the other down Sara's neck to the soft curve of her shoulder and let her fingers caress the firm flesh at the top of the camisole. With the tip of her tongue, Rebecca probed just inside Sara's lips. Sara moaned, strengthening her grip around Rebecca's waist, opening her mouth, begging Rebecca to explore it. Rebecca dipped her fingers under the fabric of Sara's camisole, until she had the smaller woman's breast clasped in the palm of her hand. Her knees weakening. Rebecca guided Sara toward the sofa, but tripped on the edge of the Persian rug under the coffee table. Giggling, the two of them dropped down on the tan leather couch without losing their grips on each other.

Rebecca maneuvered into a sitting position and pulled Sara until she was straddling her legs. Without losing their lip lock, Rebecca slid her fingers under the bottom of Sara's camisole, cupping both breasts in her hands, Sara's nipples hard against her palms. Sara pulled her face away from Rebecca's and lifted the fabric over her head, tossing the garment onto the teak coffee table. Rebecca moved one hand to Sara's back, keeping her other palm pressed against a breast. She pulled Sara close enough so she could lick the silky soft skin below Sara's tan line. Her eyes rolling back in her head, she inhaled the scent of jasmine while she dragged her tongue down to the pink areola and the hard nub in the center. Sara whimpered softly until Rebecca's tongue found her nipple. She thrust her breast toward Rebecca who was only too happy to suck on it. Sara wiggled her hips and Rebecca could smell her arousal.

Keeping the delectable flesh between her lips, Rebecca

moved her hands to the button at the waistband of Sara's slacks. When she got the zipper down, Sara pulled her breast from Rebecca's mouth, stood, and removed slacks, lavender laced panties, and sandals in one fluid motion. She returned to her position straddling Rebecca's thighs, and leaned over to kiss Rebecca's neck while reaching behind her to unzip her dress.

Rebecca let Sara pull the dress down, and off her arms, and then reach behind her to unfasten her black bra. Kissing Rebecca's shoulders, Sara slid off the straps of the bra. She followed the fabric with her lips, kissing her way across Rebecca's collarbone to her breasts. With a reverence Rebecca had never seen in a man's eyes, Sara cupped Rebecca's breasts in her hands then covered them both with kisses. Rebecca sighed with pleasure and Sara smiled. When her lips found their way around Rebecca's nipple, both women moaned.

Holding Sara's head tight against her breast with one hand, Rebecca caressed the smooth flesh over Sara's soft ass with the other. She ran her hand along Sara's outer thigh, then brought it back up between her legs to the glistening blond hairs at the top. Her fingers found their way inside the hot moist lips. When she touched Sara's clit, the woman gushed juices all over her hand. Unable to resist the musky smell any longer, Rebecca eased Sara off her lap onto the coffee table and knelt on the rug to feast on the luscious flesh, lapping up the delicious ambrosia from where it flowed freely.

Sara cried out and shuddered. She tangled her fingers in Rebecca's hair, pulling Rebecca tighter against her crotch. Rebecca lost track of how many times she made Sara come. Her own arousal had increased every time Sara had gushed and she was getting desperate for relief. Rebecca pulled her head away from the delectable folds between Sara's legs and kissed her way back up to Sara's mouth. But the younger woman dodged Rebecca's kiss and Rebecca cringed.

"Oh, that was wonderful, thank you so much." Sara kissed Rebecca's neck. "I'm just not sure ... I wouldn't know how ...

I mean, I don't know if I can return the favor."

Rebecca gritted her teeth. She stuck her arms back in the sleeves of her dress, pulling it up to cover her breasts. Wouldn't be the first time a curious straight woman used her to experiment. Now, she just needed to get Sara out of the apartment as quickly as possible so she could retreat to her bedroom and her trusty vibrator.

"No, don't, please. I want to at least try." Sara's voice was husky. "I do want to taste you. I just don't have a clue how to do what you just did to me."

Rebecca laughed away the tension that had settled in between her shoulders. "Don't worry, sweetie." She raised herself up so she could unbuckle her belt and pull her dress down over her hips, taking black cotton panties with it. "You know what feels good when someone does it to you." She sat on the sofa, her legs spread wide.

Sara nodded, her hair caressing Rebecca's breasts. She reached out and touched Rebecca's breast, running one finger around and around the nipple.

Rebecca moaned and reached for Sara's head. With one hand on the back of Sara's neck, Rebecca tugged her face down until Sara knelt in front of her and kissed the inside of first one thigh then the other. Sara stared up at Rebecca, her eyes shining with lust. "You do smell heavenly." Sara licked her way up Rebecca's leg. With her fingers, she gently parted Rebecca's outer lips and for a moment stared at the throbbing, moist, inner labia. Rebecca thought she would chicken out again, but Sara stuck out her tongue and gave Rebecca's clit a light lick. Rebecca moaned and pushed her hips toward Sara's mouth. Another half swipe of Sara's tongue left Rebecca more frustrated than anything. *Patience. Give her a chance*, she said to herself.

Rebecca put her hands under Sara's arms and pulled her face up to hers. She kissed her hard, Sara's musk mixing with a bit of her own, then stood and led her into the bedroom. Falling back on the bed, Rebecca reached for Sara's hips. Sara laid down on her side next to Rebecca with her head facing Rebecca's crotch.

Rebecca grabbed Sara's hips and tugged until Sara positioned her pussy over Rebecca's face. "Now, just do what I do." Rebecca licked the length of Sara's slit and Sara obligingly leaned forward and repeated the action. Rebecca thrust her tongue deep into Sara's pussy and gasped when Sara mimicked her. Pulling apart the folds of Sara's labia, Rebecca sucked on her clit. Sara finally positioned her lips exactly where Rebecca needed them to be and sent her over the edge. That seemed to ease Sara's inhibitions, because she lapped at the juices flowing from Rebecca with a voracious hunger that made Rebecca come again. She wrapped her arms around Sara's wonderfully soft ass and buried her face in Sara's folds. Although Sara didn't imitate Rebecca's motions precisely, her enthusiastic efforts more than satisfied Rebecca.

When the two finally stopped from exhaustion, the red rays of the setting sun poured in through the bedroom window. While Sara turned herself around so she could rest her head on Rebecca's shoulder, Rebecca glanced at the alarm clock and saw it was after nine. "Should we send Mark a thank you note?"

Sara laughed. "Nah, he'd probably just start harassing us about letting him watch and that would freak me out again."

Rebecca pulled Sara closer, wrapping her arms around her. "Forget that. I'm keeping you all to myself."

Sara stretched her arm across Rebecca's waist and one leg found its way between Rebecca's. "That works for me."

# Passion's Price

**I.G. Frederick**

Gina shifted her weight from one foot to the other and studied the passengers streaming out of SeaTac's terminal building toward waiting family members, shuttle buses, and taxi drivers. Tugging on the hem of her denim mini-skirt, she wished she had worn her usual, comfortable slacks. But Richard had told her he was a leg man and she'd promised him she had all the legs he would ever need. She didn't have much to offer above the waist, barely filling a C-cup, but she hoped he would find legs, toned through daily runs along the waterfront, to his liking. When she sent him a picture, he *had* called her cute and complimented her thick, dark hair, perky nose, and bright green eyes.

Gina's feet hurt in the brand new, two-inch high heels and she longed for her customary flat sandals. Still, if Richard appreciated her efforts, the discomfort would pay off. She leaned her weight against the door of her Mazda Miata convertible, the top down as it nearly always was when the sun broke through the ubiquitous Seattle clouds. According to the flight status monitors inside, his plane had landed twenty minutes ago. But, she couldn't see any sign of the one who had stolen her heart from three thousand miles away.

At last, a tall blond man wearing khaki slacks and a navy sport coat with dark glasses hiding his eyes, broke away from the bustling crowd and headed toward where she had parked. She twirled a long strand of ebony hair around one finger.

"Gina?"

She would recognize the way he said her name anywhere. She slid her arms around his neck, pressed herself against the length of his body, and kissed him, running her tongue along the inside of his lips. Richard's mouth tasted of spearmint. His tongue found its way into her mouth and he dropped the duffel bag he carried on the asphalt by her feet, wrapping his arms around her. Her breathing quickened and she let her hands slide down his muscular chest and slip behind his waist.

"Move along, you two," an airport security officer called out, slapping his ticket book against his palm. Gina flinched at the brusque command.

"I like the way you say hello." Richard smiled and picked up his leather duffel.

She walked around to the driver's side and popped the trunk. His bag stowed, Richard folded himself into the passenger seat and pulled the seatbelt around his broad chest. Gina put the car in gear, and Richard put his hand on her bare knee, sliding his fingers up toward the hem of her skirt. Out of the corner of one eye, she could see him smiling. She returned her attention to the roadway, watching for taxis darting in and out of traffic and airport shuttles lumbering across lanes.

"You should have sent me pictures of these. I might have flown out here sooner."

Gina had pushed for Richard to visit her in Seattle only weeks after they'd progressed from instant messaging to telephone chats. Dozens of hours-long conversations had convinced her that Richard was the man she wanted to marry. The sweetest, most considerate person she'd ever known; he had a poet's soul. They laughed at the same jokes, listened to the same music, and even shared the same sexual fantasies. Still, she had waited months until he seemed comfortable enough to take their Internet/telephone relationship to the next level. Not only had he initially refused to travel to Seattle, he also had discouraged her from flying to New York to visit him. Twice he'd tried to terminate their budding relationship, but each time he started calling her again after only a day or two.

Now he sat beside her with his hand on her thigh, the touch of his skin igniting a searing heat between her legs. As the car picked up speed, the wind tossed Gina's hair about. The noise of traffic all around them prevented the conversation into which they eased so readily on the telephone. Richard released Gina's leg and wrapped his hand in a strand of her hair. He brought it to his lips and let it caress his tanned cheek. With one hand on the wheel and the other on the stick shift, Gina couldn't respond as she wanted; she had to wait until they arrived at her apartment a few miles away. Then, they could experience for real the fantasies that had consumed her since Richard first responded to her online ad.

After parking her car in the underground garage, Gina and Richard rode the elevator to the ninth floor. Richard's arm draped over Gina's shoulder, and his cheek rested against her hair. She clasped him about the waist, gratified to finally hold the man of her dreams. Richard had contacted Gina when she sought solace online from yet another failed relationship. At thirty-six, she'd forsaken the hope of finding the love of her life. She would have settled for a man with whom she could live comfortably.

At first, Richard's interest had been titillating, but hardly practical. Too much country separated them. Gina could never leave Seattle. She'd spent her whole life there, except for four years at Columbia. Her parents, brother, and all her friends lived in the surrounding area. She couldn't abide the climate back east, or the temperament of the people. And, she knew a New Yorker would have difficulty adjusting to a Pacific Northwest lifestyle. Despite her doubts, Gina fell in love. She just had to overcome *his* doubts.

The instant the apartment door closed behind them, Gina put a hand behind Richard's neck and pulled his face to hers. She sucked his tongue into her mouth and cupped his ass in her free hand. Breathing heavily, Richard tangled his fingers in her hair with one hand and reached under her shirt, massaging her breast, with the other. He used her hair to pull her head back and pinched her hardened nipple between his thumb and forefinger, making Gina gasp. She wore only a thong under her skirt and she could feel dampness permeating the fabric. With a tug, she pulled herself free of Richard's embrace, took his hand, and led him through the living room to her bedroom. He whistled when they walked past the magnificent view of Puget Sound, the Olympic Mountains in the distance, but didn't stop to take a closer look.

Before leaving for the airport, Gina had lowered the shades in the bedroom, turned down the lights, and stretched a half dozen strands of soft, cotton rope across freshly laundered satin sheets. When his eyes found the bed, Richard inhaled sharply, a low moan emanating from his throat. He wrapped his hand in her hair again and tugged until Gina knelt in front of him. The pressure on her hair pulled her head back, forcing her to look into his eyes. The cold glint sent a shiver through her. Without relaxing his grip, Richard pushed her face toward his crotch. Obediently, she unhooked his belt and unzipped his khakis, letting them drop to the carpet. His cock protruded from his checked boxers and she pulled the elastic waistband around his erection to remove them. Gina let an appreciative gaze run from his strong muscular calves and thighs, to his slender hips and waist. She reached out, letting her fingers graze the soft skin of his cock, and kissing the swollen tip. Moving her hands around to grasp his firm buttocks, Gina slid her lips down the length of him. She had difficulty taking all of him in her mouth and concentrated on breathing through her nose. Richard moaned, never releasing the grip on her hair, while she eased his cock in and out.

His hips moved in a rhythm that forced her to increase the pace. Her eyes widened as she struggled not to gag. Richard pushed himself into her harder and harder until he suddenly stopped, her chin against his balls, moaning while he shot warm semen down her throat. For a few moments he stood there, his hand still tightly wrapped in her hair. Then, he tugged until she found her way to her feet.

"Take off your clothes." His voice had a husky quality that sent another shiver down Gina's spine.

He still held her by the hair, her head tilted back. Gina reached behind her waist and unzipped her mini skirt and pushed it over her hips. Slowly, she unbuttoned her blouse, pulled it off her shoulders, and let it drop to the floor with the rest of their clothing. She unhooked her lacy black bra, dropped it, and stuck her thumbs inside the strings of her thong.

"That's enough." Richard pulled her over to the bed by her hair, and tossed her face down. In matter of minutes, he had her hands tied at the wrist behind her back. He bent her legs at the knee, and bound her ankles to her thighs, the spiked heels pointing toward her elbows. Lisa squirmed, but his knots held firm. He flipped her over on her back and used another piece of rope to bind her breasts. Standing back for a moment, his gaze wandered over his handiwork. He removed his jacket and shirt, his eyes never leaving Gina's body.

When he stood before her naked, he slid his hands from her knees to her thighs, inhaling deeply. Leaning down, Richard nuzzled her thong out of the way with his nose and pushed his mouth into her dripping pussy. Gina squirmed again in her bindings, the movement increasing the pressure of the rope around her tits. A low growl periodically escaped his throat while Richard licked, sucked, and nibbled her. Gina could only concentrate on the exquisite tension in her clit. When she exploded, the tremor travelled the length of her body. Richard kissed his way up her belly to her breasts, biting each one hard before kissing her. She tasted her own juices, pungent on his mouth and tongue.

Helping himself to one of the condoms in the bowl Gina had left on the nightstand, Richard knelt between her thighs. When he drove into her, she cried out. The intensity of pleasure overwhelmed her and Gina found herself only surreally aware of her surroundings. Her skin burned everywhere it touched Richard. He invaded her senses, the bristly blond hair on his chest, the strength in his arms, the graceful length of his fingers tangled in her hair.

Richard pounded against her and Gina moaned. The force of his thrusts caused the rope to chafe against her skin and she revelled in the sensory overload. Thrusting faster and harder, he slammed into her, grunting with pleasure. Gina couldn't move or speak, she just lay beneath him letting the building excitement consume her. She exploded again. Never before had a man given her this much pleasure.

When he shuddered with a loud groan, Gina smiled. Even though they had confided their most intimate secrets on the telephone, Richard had always contended that the success of their relationship would depend on chemistry. Surely, he had no doubts now.

℘

When Richard returned to New York eight days later, Gina had extracted his promise that he would move to Seattle. Assured of the inevitability of their union, she saw no reason to wait. Richard had lost his job as a computer programmer a few weeks before his trip. She questioned why he would seek a position that would keep him in New York. Although Seattle had a higher unemployment rate, surely with his experience and her contacts, he would have no trouble finding work. And he wouldn't have to worry about paying rent if he lived with her.

Gina tried to help with the move as much as possible. She flew to New York and furiously packed boxes for two days. She tried to get Richard to divest himself of some things rather than move them -- mismatched dishes, odd utensils, dented pots and pans. She owned top-of-the-line cookware and six-piece Dansk place settings for twelve. Richard insisted he wanted to bring it all, so Gina packed everything, even the torn shirt and the broken cup.

Things fell into place until they rented the U-Haul. Returning from the office to his apartment, they discovered one of the truck's taillights didn't work. Richard had to maneuver the vehicle, with the tow-dolly pulling his car, back through heavy Brooklyn traffic. By the time they returned with another truck, a rainstorm had started and water dripped inside the van.

When they returned yet again to the U-Haul office, Gina released the fury that had been building all week. "How can you rent out vehicles that aren't in operable condition?" she demanded of the clerk. "This is the second truck we've had to return. You should give us a brand new truck and a discounted rate. We've already lost a day of travel because of this." Gina had arranged for Richard to meet with an employment specialist in Seattle on Monday. They had planned to be back by Saturday giving them a day to unload and return the truck before he started job hunting. Now they'd have to push to get in by Sunday night.

"Perhaps we could postpone Monday's appointment," Richard said quietly while the clerk looked in the computer for another truck.

"That's ridiculous. We shouldn't have to rearrange our schedule because these people refuse to maintain their fleet." Although she loved how Richard treated everyone he encountered with impeccable courtesy, sometimes Gina thought he carried politeness too far. As a result, others probably assumed they could take advantage of him.

Gina turned to the clerk. "What's taking so long? We've

lost a full day on this nonsense already. Don't you have any trucks that don't need repair?"

"Gina, sweetie." Richard tilted his head to one side, looking at the crooked nameplate on the clerk's uniform. "Alisha here's just trying to do her job."

"Don't be ridiculous. If she did her job, we wouldn't have needed to come back here twice with trucks that weren't fit to drive across town, never mind across the country. I just can't wait to see what piece of junk they try to foist on us next."

"The only fourteen-foot truck available to drive to Seattle is on Hillsdale in Jamaica." Alisha looked at Richard.

"Queens!?!?" Gina approached the end of her patience. "How the hell long will it take us to get over there?" Richard didn't even need a truck that big. What he owned would easily fit into a ten-footer. But none of the trucking companies would rent anything smaller with a dolly to tow his car. Gina didn't want to drive across the country in separate vehicles.

"How late is the office in Jamaica open?" Richard asked.

"Until five." Alisha punched some more keys and squinted at the screen. "I could call and ask them to wait for you, but you'd need to leave now."

"Thank you, Alisha." Richard took Gina's arm. "At this time of day, we need at least forty-five minutes, maybe an hour to drive over there. Otherwise, we won't have any truck at all."

With reluctance, Gina let Richard lead her back to the parking lot rather than insist that the clerk find someone to bring the truck to them.

☞

"Gina, I can't live like this," Richard announced four days after they'd unloaded the truck and moved all his belongings into her apartment. He lay at the far edge of the bed, one arm protecting his eyes from the morning sun seeping in along the edges of the shades.

The whirlwind of activity that had consumed the past few weeks finally over, Gina looked forward to settling down to her new life with Richard. His statement left her gasping for breath. "What do you mean?"

"I can't live with you. I've had doubts from the beginning. I never should have let you talk me into moving out here."

Nausea punched Gina in her stomach. Between her airline ticket, the rental truck, hotels and meals on the road, and gasoline, she had spent almost five thousand dollars moving Richard to Seattle, most of her savings.

"What's wrong, Richard?" With difficulty, Gina kept her voice steady.

Richard sighed. "You're too intense. You've taken over my life."

"I thought I was helping. You seemed so overwhelmed by everything that needed to be done."

After they returned from New York, Gina had plunged back into her regular routine. Rising at five, she ran for forty-five minutes, showered, grabbed a latté, and arrived at the office by seven-thirty. She'd scheduled dinners and lunches so Richard could meet all her friends, as well as some of her many contacts who worked in tech jobs.

"You know," Richard said, "I lived in New York City, but I paced my life slower and with less pressure than yours."

Gina blinked rapidly, fighting back tears. "It seems a little much right now, what with the move and trying to find a job. You'll see; everything will be fine."

"I don't think so, Gina. You're a drama queen. Even a stubbed toe rates an emotional outburst. I can't live like that."

She swallowed and glanced at the clock. "I'm late. I'll try to leave work early tonight. We can talk more at dinner."

℞

Three days later, Richard moved out. He'd gotten a job placement through a temporary agency, put most of his belongings into storage, and taken a room at the Y. Gina wept the entire weekend. She went to work on Monday, still numb. When colleagues commented about her red eyes, she blamed allergies. She told no one about Richard leaving, not even her closest friends. They had derided her for moving too fast, for bringing into her home a man she met on the Internet only a few months before. If they knew how much money she'd spent, they'd berate her for months.

When anyone suggested plans to get together with Gina and Richard, she made excuses. Each night she returned to her empty apartment and sat in front of the television. She paid no attention to what flickered on the screen. Some nights, she forgot to turn it on.

In the months that followed, friends made comments about Richard taking all Gina's time, but they no longer suggested getting together for lunch, dinner, or a concert. Gina had pulled her ad from the personals website shortly after she and Richard started talking on the telephone. She never bothered to re-post it. After convincing herself she'd found her soul mate in Richard, she was unable to venture into the emotional landmine of another relationship.

Work became her panacea. She found pleasure in developing new accounts and creating ingenious ways to solve problems, spending more and more time at the office, even weekends.

Two days after she was promoted to a supervisory position, Richard called. "I've missed you, Gina."

She sat on her sofa, holding the telephone in her hand, staring at it.

"Are you there?"

She heard his voice as if in the distance and put the phone back to her ear. "Yes."

"I thought maybe we could get together for an evening. I think one of the problems I had is that we moved too fast. We went from talking on the telephone to living together. We never had a chance to date, to get to know each other."

True enough, Gina thought. But, did it matter now? With reluctance, she agreed to meet Richard for dinner Friday night.

Preparing for work that Friday morning, she debated about what to wear. The two-inch heels, unworn since Richard moved out, still rested in their Nordstrom's box. Gina left them and dressed in her usual tailored business suit, with below-the-knee skirt. She chose sensible, low-heeled pumps.

Her heart caught in her throat when she walked toward the table and Richard rose from his seat, holding out the chair next to his. Although he had on a jacket, his blue shirt was unbuttoned at the collar and he didn't wear a tie. She doubted if he would have dressed as casually to dine at one of New York's finest restaurants. Apparently, he'd adapted quickly to the Seattle lifestyle. Gina slipped off her own jacket and draped it over the seat back. Richard kissed her neck.

Gina's internal debate about whether or not she wanted Richard back made it difficult to concentrate on what he said. Later, she vaguely remembered him telling her that he'd found a contract position at Microsoft and an apartment in Bellevue. She forgot what she'd shared with him about her life, whether she even mentioned the promotion. Richard returned to the apartment with her. Gina couldn't recall if she had invited him.

They sat on the couch in the living room, watching the lights of the ferries crossing the Sound. Richard took her hand in hers. "Has there been anyone else, Gina?"

She shook her head and Richard kissed each finger, one at a time. "I hoped you'd say that. I haven't seen anyone since I left, either." His lips traveled slowly along the inside of her arm to her neck and up to her face. With their lips locked together, Gina's arms found their way around Richard's neck of their own accord. Their tongues danced. His hand moved along her thigh, to her hip, and found its way to her breast. He pinched her nipple. Her breath came in heavy rasps, but Gina made no other sound.

One hand tangled in her hair, pulling her head back, Richard deftly undid the buttons of her blouse. The broadcloth of the couch felt rough against her bare skin. After he removed her bra and used it to tie her hands behind her back, Richard kissed a moist trail from her mouth to her breast. He sucked on her nipple, teasing it with his teeth, while his fingers unhooked the fastenings of her skirt. Gina lifted her hips so he could pull it, along with her underwear and pantyhose, out of his way. Then, his mouth explored her belly, the inside of her thighs, and her nether lips.

Gina's body responded to his sensual touch, but her mind watched as if from a distance. Oblivious to her aloofness, Richard sucked her clit and thrust his tongue into her pussy until she finally trembled with orgasm. Then he kissed his way back to her mouth, stood, and removed his clothing. Part of Gina wanted him, but she couldn't be sure if *any* attractive man would have addressed that need.

Panting, Richard slipped one arm under her shoulders and the other under her knees. He lifted her from the couch and carried her to the bedroom, hesitating only a few seconds when he saw the unmade bed. Since he left, Gina had let things go in the apartment. Dishes piled up in the sink, laundry was heaped in the corner, and she rarely made the bed anymore.

The cotton sheets against her back cooled her heated skin, and helped clear her mind. Gina considered asking Richard to leave. But the touch of his hands on her ass, his firm chest muscles pressed against her breasts, and his stiff cock between her thighs ignited a fire within her. When he entered her, it felt so very good. She let him find his own rhythm, the weight of his thrusts pressing her hands into the small of her back. Although she came twice, she remained silent.

Richard stayed between her legs long after he climaxed, kissing her and stroking her hair. When he rolled to his side, he pressed against her, one arm still beneath her neck, the other stretched under her breasts.

"What's wrong, Gina?" He reached behind her and removed the bra that bound her wrists.

She didn't answer, wondering if she wanted Richard back, and if she could remove the drama from her life to keep him. She certainly had found little to get excited about these past few months.

"You used to be so passionate during sex." He took one nipple in his mouth and bit down hard enough to make Gina gasp.

"You said you couldn't live with drama, that I was too intense. You can't have passion without drama and intensity." She rolled out from under his arm and to her feet. "Maybe you were right to leave." Looking down at the man in her bed, Gina realized she knew more about him than anyone other than herself. On the telephone, they'd confided without restraint. She'd never tried to hide her passion for life, had thought he found it appealing.

"I realize now that you're not a drama queen, Gina. You just approach things differently than I do." Richard sat up and stretched his arms toward her. Gina stayed out of reach. "I'm not sure I can get used to the way you live, but I want to try. I miss you. I miss talking to you every day, sharing everything. When I got the job at Microsoft, my first thought was 'Gina will be so excited.' Then I realized you didn't even know that I'd applied, that I'd gotten a second interview, that they were checking my references. I was so disappointed."

Richard stood, walked to Gina, and wrapped his arms around her. Gina stayed still, her hands at her sides. "We got a rough start, Gina. Too much happened too fast. Me losing my job, not having any money or a place to live, didn't help. I was hoping you'd consider starting all over again, but taking it slow this time." He tilted her chin up with his fingers and stared at her with intense blue eyes.

"I know I never told you I loved you. I'm not even sure when I did fall in love with you. But I've realized since I've been gone just how much you mean to me. Now that I'm back on my feet, I want to find a way for us to make a life together. Please, Gina, give me another chance."

Gina felt a tear drifting from the corner of her eye down her cheek. Richard leaned down and licked it off. His lips found hers and she let her arms slip around his waist.

# Lunchtime Lover

## I.G. Frederick

Lisa shifted closer, nestling her head on Collin's shoulder and throwing a leg over his thigh. She let the waves of post-orgasmic throbbing wash over her while he ran his fingers through her hair and the heat of his skin enveloped her. Her hand wandered over the well-defined muscles of his chest, and a contented sigh slipped out.

Her mind wandered to the work she needed to complete as soon as Collin left. During the past few weeks, instead of rushing back to the office, he had stayed longer and longer. Normally, she appreciated the extra attention. Now that her divorce was final, she could enjoy Collin's clandestine, twice-weekly visits without guilt. But this afternoon deadlines loomed and Lisa needed to encourage Collin to leave.

"Lisa." He dragged one finger up her arm and along her neck, sending a shiver down her spine.

"Mmmm."

"I've decided I can't do this anymore."

Lisa bolted upright and stared down at the tall, lean man

stretched the length of her bed, his skin pale against the dark blue sheets. "What? Why?" She folded her arms under her breasts, gripping her biceps with her fingers. Had Collin found someone else, or had the guilt of betraying his own spouse caught up with him? Lisa would never have survived the past several months without Collin. He had provided the life raft of stability during the storm that ended her twelve-year marriage. Collin also had offered an amazing boost to her self-esteem -- nothing like a younger lover to take away the bitter sting of a husband who suddenly found you unattractive.

Collin reached up and pulled her back into his arms, kissing her forehead and running one hand slowly up and down her back. She looked into his eyes, hoping to lose herself in the jolt his gaze always sent through her and forget that he might not spend anymore leisurely lunch hours in her bed. Lisa had never figured out which turned her on more, the square chin, the full lips, or the ever-changing color of Collin's hazel eyes. Running her fingers through his silky dark brown hair, she pulled his mouth to meet hers.

He resisted. "Sneaking over here ... making excuses at work ... worrying about Audrey finding out... I can't anymore." He shook his head.

*Rats*, Lisa thought. She just didn't have the time to invest in finding another lover now, and she'd reached the point in her life when she found her raging libido extremely distracting. She sighed, pushed herself free of Collin's embrace, and rolled off the other side of the bed. Picking out her own clothing from the pile on the floor, she headed for the bathroom, the wooden floorboards chilly against her bare feet. She'd have to finish the CBU project before she could even think of going online to look for Collin's replacement. And no telling how long that would take. He'd answered her ad the day after she posted it, but they'd spent weeks getting to know each other over e-mail and the telephone before that first, hesitant meeting for coffee.

Lisa set her clothes on top of the toilet lid and turned on the water in the shower. If she skipped her long lunch hours with Collin, she could have the bulk of the CBU work done and ready for Larry to review by the end of next week. That would give her a holiday weekend to post ads on the most promising sites. Maybe this time she would find someone she could date openly.

Collin stood in the doorway, his arms crossed in front of a chest covered with black hair. He pursed his lips and pulled his eyebrows together. "Don't you even want to know what I plan to do?"

Lisa stepped into the shower, pulled the glass door closed behind her, and let the hot water flow over her face and onto her shoulders. "I figure you'll tell me if you want me to know."

At first, Lisa had agonized about having an affair with the husband of a woman confined to a wheelchair. But she'd assuaged her guilt with the knowledge that after three years Audrey hadn't regained the ability to enjoy sex. And with her own marriage falling apart, Lisa had desperately needed the solace she found in Collin's arms. She closed her eyes for a moment, letting the hot water course down her face. Single now, she should be able to manage her life without Collin's support. Lisa reached for the washcloth. Time she started looking for someone who could be more than a lunchtime lover.

Pulling open the shower door, Collin stepped into the stream of hot water and took the washcloth from Lisa's hands. He held it above her head until it was wet and then reached around her for the soap. She let him wash her back, even though she knew they would end up with soap-slippery bodies entwined together on the tile floor. Work could wait while she enjoyed their last time together.

Collin lowered himself to his knees. He washed her breasts with the reverent look he always had on his face during foreplay. His arms slipped around her and his head nestled against her chest. The washcloth forgotten, he slid soap-slick hands down her back, stopping to cup her ass and squeeze before moving down her outer thighs and calves. When he reached her ankles, Collin moved his hands inside and they glided back up. Weak-kneed, Lisa ran her fingers through his wet hair, using her touch on his head to keep from losing her equilibrium.

When he reached the top of her legs, Collin nudged her into a wider stance and burrowed his face inside her. She cried out and grabbed the ceramic soap dish attached to the wall for support. The trembling started in her toes and worked its way up her body until she could no longer stand. She lowered herself to her knees and Collin embraced her while the hot water cascaded over them. Her hands explored his arms, back, ass while he crushed her breasts against his chest and squeezed her ass cheeks in his hands.

With a practiced move, Collin stretched his legs out under her and pulled Lisa into his lap. Still on her knees, she moved up and down in the steaming shower, lost in the delicious sensation of fullness while he plunged in and out of her. She concentrated on the building tension riding the wave to orgasm after orgasm before Collin bellowed, gripping her tightly.

They kissed, tongues dancing together and arms wrapped around each other until the throbbing eased and Collin slipped out.

"I'm going to leave Audrey."

Eyes wide, Lisa stared at the stranger who'd appeared in her shower.

"I mean it. I can't stand sneaking over here during lunch anymore. I want to come home to you every night. I love you, Lisa. I want to marry you."

Lisa used Collin's shoulders to push herself to a standing position. She found the washcloth and finished her interrupted cleansing, trying to absorb the meaning of his words. From the beginning, they'd promised each other that falling in love wasn't an option. Lisa had yet to recover from discovering her husband's affair with another woman. Collin swore that he only needed a physical relationship -- he still loved Audrey and would never leave her.

He sat on the shower floor while she scrubbed her skin with the soapy washcloth. When she finished, she handed him the cloth, pulled the shower wand from its holder, and rinsed off.

Not until she'd toweled dry and pulled on her clothing was Lisa composed enough to speak. "Collin, you always said this relationship would never be more than an affair -- that you wouldn't leave your wife. I took you at your word." Lisa sighed. She should have recognized Collin's growing affection. Although she'd seen the symptoms, the distraction of work had kept her too busy to make the connection.

Collin slicked the water off his chest and arms with his hands before stepping out and reaching for a towel. "I didn't count on falling in love with you." His voice was husky.

"I'm not in love with you." Whenever she'd yearned for an emotional commitment with Collin, Lisa reminded herself that he could have an affair behind his wife's back. Now she wondered if she *could* learn to love him.

"Of course you aren't." He rubbed himself with the towel and Lisa resisted an urge to let her fingers follow its path. She would miss his strong arms, that wonderfully squeezable rear, and her ability to share almost any thought with him. "You didn't think I was available. I know you've held yourself in check, kept your emotions bottled up inside." He reached for her, but she stepped aside.

*Such gall!* Lisa took a deep breath and shook her head. "No, Collin. I could never fall in love with you. I'd never want any more involvement with you than what I have now." Although she spoke the words, Lisa wondered if she could live them.

Collin stood slack-jawed, and the towel dropped from his fingers onto the floor. "But why, Lisa? We like the same things. We enjoy being together. And, you must admit, the sex has been amazing."

Lisa combed the tangles out of her hair. She assessed her appearance, remembering how she'd worded the online ad Collin had answered. "Perky, brunette with green eyes and big tits..." If she wanted more than a lunchtime lover, she should emphasize something besides her physical attributes. And maybe she shouldn't be looking for a mate online. She chastised her reflection. *Home wrecker!* She had blamed Bradley's infidelity for ending their marriage. But she regularly made love to a man she knew had a wife waiting at home for him in a wheelchair. And now Collin wanted to leave Audrey and marry her. She thought what life could be like as Collin's wife. With his income, she could cut back on the hours she worked, no longer struggle to make the house payments.

Still .... Lisa caught Collin's eye in the mirror. "Great sex isn't the best foundation for a relationship. If something happens to one of you ... ." She thought of the drunk driver who had left Audrey paralyzed below the waist.

Collin stepped up behind Lisa and wrapped his arms around her shoulders. He smelled only of soap, his scent and hers washed away to protect their secret. When he pressed his lips against the side of her neck, his breath tickled her skin. "No, but as you know firsthand, without sex, a relationship really can't last, either."

Lisa pressed her lips together, but didn't respond. She pulled Collin's hands apart and stepped out of his embrace. "I have work to do." She went downstairs to her office.

"I thought you'd be happy about my decision." Collin stood to one side of her desk, buttoning his shirt and tucking it into his pants.

"Maybe you should have checked with me first. I liked the arrangement just fine the way it was." She thumbed through the CBU documents, looking for the spreadsheet she'd used to organize the statistics collected during the past two weeks.

Turning in her chair, Lisa looked up at Collin. Damn, she'd miss him, but she needed to send him back to his wife. "Look, Collin, I like you a lot. Really I do. And yes, the sex has been fantastic. But I don't love you and I'll never love you. And even if I did, I'd never consider marrying you."

His upper lip twitched and Collin blinked rapidly. He slouched into the chair in front of the desk and pouted. "Why?"

Lisa turned again to face him, leaned her forearms on the desk, and stared straight into Collin's eyes. They took on the color of whatever shirt he wore, so now they had a bluish cast. "Because I could never trust you."

He sat up straight and stared at her.

"I may have started having sex with you when I was still legally married, but my relationship with Bradley had ended." Lisa filed for divorce when she found her husband with his twenty-five-year-old secretary. "I would never have gotten intimate with you if I'd any hope of a reconciliation with Bradley. I know Audrey can't meet your physical needs. But, I don't respect your decision to have an affair, even though I've been the beneficiary of that choice." She sat back in her chair. "I could never believe any commitment you made. I'd always be wondering if you were looking for a little on the side when I wasn't around. Once an adulterer, always an adulterer." That statement could apply to herself, and she wondered if she would find a man who could trust *her*.

"But, but, Lisa." Collin turned the "a" at the end of her name into a whine.

"I have a lot of work to do, Collin. I think you'd better go back to the office."

"What about Friday?"

"It's probably best if you stop coming over here on your lunch hour." Lisa found the spreadsheet and started checking the printout data against her notes. Collin didn't move. She tried to forget him, and concentrate on the numbers.

When he finally rose, Collin walked out of the room

without his usual goodbye kiss and trite "'til next time, love" proclamation. Lisa wondered if he'd told Audrey yet or if he could still go home. Regardless, she expected to see him online, trolling for another lunchtime lover, within a matter of days. She heard the front door open and close and put her head down on the desk, waiting for the tears to start. She blinked several times, her eyes dry, and sat up.

Although he'd offered comfort during her distress, the relationship had been based on sex. Collin had filled a need in her life. As much as she tried to convince herself that she could accept a purely physical relationship, Lisa realized now that she wanted more from a man. She needed someone who could be her friend and companion as well as her lover. Taking a deep breath, she returned to her work.

# Acknowledgements

This book would not have reached your hands without the help of many dear friends and colleagues. I thank my readers and supporters, especially Cindy, my proofreader, editor, and best friend. Thanks also to all those who have served me, well and ill, over the years. I have learned something from each one of you and I hope that you find what you seek.

*Other fiction*
**by I.G. Frederick includes:**

# Cougar Conquests

**Beautiful older women on the prowl and the sweet young cubs captured by their allure**

*"Benjamin"* — *A chance meeting at a munch in a tiny town leads Benjamin to an opportunity for training. But, Lady Gina tries to end the relationship rather than emotionally torture herself.*

*"Festival of Eros"* — *The handsome young man followed her around all evening, behaving like the perfect submissive ... until she learned his identity.*

*"Paddles"* — *A biker bar with no bikers? The decor, name, and patrons of a bar in a small Eastern Oregon town puzzle William who just stopped in for a beer. Then the owner introduces him to the secrets of this very special tavern.*

*"Starting Over"* - *When her pet walked out on her, she stayed away from parties because it hurt to watch other women playing with their toys. But, a friend coerces her into attending a unique event.*

*"The Cougar and the College Boys"* — *Alone in the woods, hours from Portland, Tess discovers four college friends staying in a nearby cabin. The boys invite her to share their campfire, their dinner, and ...*

www.eroticawriter.net/CougarConquests.html

*Dommemoir*

# WARNING:
### This book changes women's attitudes about relationship dynamics, forever.

*In Geneviéve's journey of discovery she dabbles in the BDSM lifestyle which forces her to recognize and acknowledge her true nature. Her memoir, woven together with that of a male slave, draws the reader into an intense odyssey of sexual expression triumphing over sexual repression while delivering fascinating insight about a different kind of love.*

*"The aptly titled* Dommemoir *delivers on so many levels... It quickly sucks you in and envelopes you in the bondage of its spell...* Dommemoir *is a character study that breathes complex and compelling life into its hero, the devastating Lady Geneviéve and the fortunate submissives who worship at her feet... placing you in the delicious bondage of its dark and compelling landscape..."*

**Larry Brooks, USA Today bestselling author of**
*Darkness Bound* **and** *Bait and Switch*

### www.eroticawriter.net/Dommemoir.html

# Eleanor & Mick

## A journey of sexual exploration and insight

In five sizzling hot stories, Eleanor seeks refuge in a small town on the Oregon Coast and befriends her younger neighbor. He captures first her heart and then her submission, taking her on a journey of sexual exploration and insight.

"Salt for His Wounds" — When Eleanor's ex-husband shows up begging for a second chance, she asks her young, gorgeous next door neighbor for a favor and Mick takes advantage of the opportunity.

"The Mercantile" — Eleanor attributes Mick's detachment to the difference in their ages, but Mick confesses a need for kink. Afraid of losing him, Eleanor reluctantly consents to bondage and pain.

"The Things We Do for Love" — When her gorgeous girlfriend visits Eleanor on the coast, Mick's obvious attraction troubles her. But, Liz only has eyes for Eleanor.

"Paid in Full" — Mick's army buddy finds Eleanor hot and makes a deal with Mick. But, if Mick really loved Eleanor would he let another man have sex with her?

"Renovations" — After Mick spends a month renovating their garage, Eleanor discovers he built in a few surprises.

www.eroticawriter.net/EleanorMick.html

# Family Dynamics

## Six sultry stories exploring sexuality in Dominant/submissive liaisons

*"'Aunt' Grace"* — *Jen needed a place to stay in Portland and turned to her father's stepsister. But, she found so much more than she ever dreamed possible with her "Aunt" Grace. Second Place, NLA:I John Preston Short Story Award.*

*"Leather Family"* — *Kyle needs his own boy. Jacques would do almost anything to find a place in a Leather Family. But, Kyle serves a female Master.*

*"Searching"* — *Two dominants love each other, but need someone who submits to them both. Just how far will young Jeremy go to serve the lovely Lady Theresa?*

*"Taking Control"* — *To free the woman she loves from a horrid sadist's perverted games, Melanie must set aside her own aversion to men.*

*"Family Ties"* — *When her slave's ex faces eviction, Katherine offers refuge. But can Naomi pay the price?*

*"Said the Unicorn"* — *Tessa dedicates herself to her Master's service, so his determination to add another woman to their family devastates her.*

www.eroticawriter.net/FamilyDynamics.html

# Fork In The Road:

## Changing people's lives, and relationships in three pairs of sexy stories

"*Said the Unicorn*" — *Tessa dedicates herself to her Master's service, so his determination to add another woman to their family devastates her.*

"*Proposals*" — *The evening appears perfectly arranged for him to pop the question. But, Christopher's proposition takes Geraldine on an unanticipated sexual adventure.*

"*Winners & Losers*" — *When he finally walks away from the blackjack table, Jeffrey finds someone worth gambling on.*

**www.eroticawriter.net/ForkinRoad.html**

# Ladies in Love

## Six sizzling stories of Lesbian Lust

"Empty Seat" — Laura offers Alex a nightcap as thanks for help with a presentation to a prospective client. But they never order drinks.

"'Aunt' Grace" — Jen needed a place to stay in Portland and turned to her father's stepsister. But, she found so much more than she ever dreamed possible with her "Aunt" Grace. Second Place, NLA:I John Preston Short Story Award.

"Spa Date" — Dismayed that she introduced Sam to the woman who betrayed her, Julie tries to fix her up again.

"Taking Control" — To free the woman she loves from a horrid sadist's perverted games, Melanie must set aside her own aversion to men.

"Dental School" — How can Cindy flirt with the beautiful blonde dental instructor while her mother propositions the student examining her teeth on Cindy's behalf?

"Commiserate" — The same man dumped them both. When they commiserate, they discover more in common than an ex-boyfriend.

www.eroticawriter.net/LadiesinLove.html

# Lessons Learned

## Sometimes you need more than love

*Four sizzling hot FemDom love stories about women who come to terms with their dominant sides and discover that makes them more attractive to the men they love.*

*"Tea Party" — What if the first time your best friend drags you to a FemDom "Tea Party" you see your former boyfriend serving canapes naked?*

*"Blind Date" — How do you respond when you find your ex-husband hanging out at the restaurant where you planned to meet your "Blind Date"?*

*"To Serve" — If you love a vanilla woman and you only want "To Serve," how do you introduce her to the lifestyle without scaring her away?*

*"Change in View" — What if a "Change in View" alters the attitude of the man you mentored so he could find his perfect Mistress?*

**www.eroticawriter.net/LessonsLearned.html**

# Love Hurts

### but in a good way
### five steamy stories about the dark side of love

"B&D Trainee" —Online, Xavier promised to make his B&D fantasies come true. But, had he jumped in over his head?

"Knife Play" — Seeking a knife he saw online, Jack inadvertently found himself in a room full of pain and bondage contraptions. He almost turned around and left, but a beautiful woman taught him a different way to appreciate blades.

"Pussy Whipped" — Eric knew nothing about BDSM, but purchased a ticket to a fundraiser to help out his friends. When Miranda asks him to "play," he discovers exactly what those four letters mean.

"The Auction" —He attended the auction with only one goal — to acquire a very special whip. But an offer to try it out proved irresistible and he discovered sometimes events, and women, can exceed one's expectations.

"FemDom Fairy Tale" — A FemDom's offhand remark about a photograph at an erotic art show draws a handsome man's attention. But, when two dominants find each other attractive, which one chooses to kneel?

**www.eroticawriter.net/LoveHurts.html**

# Second Chances

## Six sexy stories about getting a second shot at the gold ring

"Back to School" — An admin error forces Jordan and Dennis to share a dorm room. Older than their classmates, they decide to stick together. But Jordan's past threatens to keep them apart.

"Gordon" — When the cover model of her latest book walks into the coffee shop where she writes, Lenore embarrassingly calls him by her character's name. His reaction confounds her.

"Spa Date" — Dismayed that she introduced Sam to the woman who betrayed her, Julie tries to fix her up again.

"Salt for His Wounds" — When Eleanor's ex-husband shows up begging for a second chance, she asks her young, gorgeous next door neighbor for a favor. Mick takes advantage of the opportunity.

"Proposal — Tangled Webs" — The evening appears perfectly arranged for him to pop the question. But, Christopher's proposition takes Geraldine on an unanticipated sexual adventure.

"Starting Over" — When her pet walked out on her, she stayed away from parties because it hurt to watch other women playing with their toys. But, a friend coerces her into attending a unique event.

www.eroticawriter.net/SecondChances.html

# When Two's Not Enough

## Seven sexy ménage stories

"Tribal Fusion" — *Whenever and wherever he dances, Dominic collects propositions, but the Lady Lenore's proposal takes him by surprise.*

"Two Brothers" — *A divorcée in a flashy sports car attracts the attention of two young virgin brothers visiting the "big" city of Boise.*

"Honeymoon" — *Although she expected to honeymoon aboard a cruise ship, Allison finds herself sailing on a private yacht staffed by an incredibly beautiful couple. Believing her new husband wants to hide his older, less attractive wife, makes it difficult to enjoy the hedonistic delights offered in paradise.*

"Jail Bait" — *Serena wants Joshua to pop her cherry, but he won't touch her because of her age. When her birthday finally makes it legal, he arranges for a very special celebration.*

*"Nikki's Birthday"* — *Even someone happy in a monogamous relationship might find the gift of a hot, new toy for an evening of decadence incredibly exciting. (Inspired by a real birthday present given to a lovely little bi-sexual, genderqueer slave.)*

*"Market Boy"* — *When a beautiful Domme offers Jack the opportunity to serve at a party for her friends, he responds too quickly and too eagerly, getting more than he bargained for.*

*"The Cougar and the College Boys"* — *Alone in the woods, hours from Portland, Tess discovers four college friends staying in a nearby cabin. The boys invite her to share their campfire, their dinner, and ...*

www.eroticawriter.net/TwoNotEnough.html

# Young & Eager

**Barely legal but hardly innocent**

*"Two Brothers"* — *A divorcée in a flashy sports car attracts the attention of two young virgin brothers visiting the "big" city of Boise.*

*"Teachers Pet"* — *Trapped at an all-girls' school in the middle of nowhere, Sabrina tries to get her hunky teacher to bust her cherry.*

*"Arresting Development"* — *Bethany went out with Officer Rick to avoid a speeding ticket, but discovered she enjoyed getting "arrested."*

*"Jail Bait"* — *Serena wants Joshua to pop her cherry, but he won't touch her because of her age. When her birthday finally makes it legal, he arranges for a very special celebration.*

**www.eroticawriter.net/YoungEager.html**

Or visit
http://eroticawriter.net/
to find links to individual stories
and additional collections
and

www.ingramcontent.com/pod-product-compliance
Lightning Source LLC
Chambersburg PA
CBHW061454170626
46811CB00004B/1502